THE PATH OF

by Harriet Brundle

The Potato Patch

BEARPORT
PUBLISHING

Minneapolis, Minnesota

Credits

All images are courtesy of Shutterstock.com, unless otherwise specified.
With thanks to Getty Images, Thinkstock Photo, and iStockphoto.

Cover images – MuchMania, PEEKABU Zentangle Gita Kulinitch Studio.
Recurring images – MuchMania, PEEKABU Zentangle Gita Kulinitch Studio,
oticki, Rimma Rii, Vanatchanan. 6 - Elena Masiutkina. 7 - Gorbenko Olena.
8 - Foto Para T. 9 - alicja neumiler. 10 - FotoDuets. 10&11 - Andrii Bezvershenko.
11 - Madlen. 12 - Matauw. 13 - Marijs, Standret. 14 - Lertwit Sasipreyajun. 15
– Ruud Morijn Photographer. 16 - EQRoy, darksoul72. 17 - 279photo Studio. 18 -
jc.space. 18&19 - Dukesn. 19 - Ghina photography. 20 - margouillat photo, Cora
Mueller. 21 - StockImageFactory.com, Fascinadora. 22&23 - Annie Lahairoy S.

Library of Congress Cataloging-in-Publication Data

Names: Brundle, Harriet, author.
Title: The path of potatoes / by Harriet Brundle.
Description: Fusion books. | Minneapolis, MN : Bearport Publishing Company,
  [2022] | Series: Drive thru | Includes bibliographical references and
  index.
Identifiers: LCCN 2021011429 (print) | LCCN 2021011430 (ebook) | ISBN
  9781647479480 (library binding) | ISBN 9781647479565 (paperback) | ISBN
  9781647479640 (ebook)
Subjects: LCSH: Potatoes--Juvenile literature. | Cooking
  (Potatoes)--Juvenile literature.
Classification: LCC SB211.P8 B865 2022 (print) | LCC SB211.P8 (ebook) |
  DDC 635/.21--dc23
LC record available at https://lccn.loc.gov/2021011429
LC ebook record available at https://lccn.loc.gov/2021011430

For more information, write to Bearport Publishing, 5357 Penn Avenue South,
Minneapolis, MN 55419. Printed in the United States of America.

CONTENTS

HOP IN THE POTATO PATCH

Hi! My name is Anna, and this is my food truck, the Potato Patch! Which potato treat would you like to try?

＊ MENU ＊

Baked potato
with cheese

French fries

Hash browns

THE PATH OF POTATOES

Potatoes are grown around the world. In the United States, potatoes are grown more than any other vegetable.

The Potato Patch

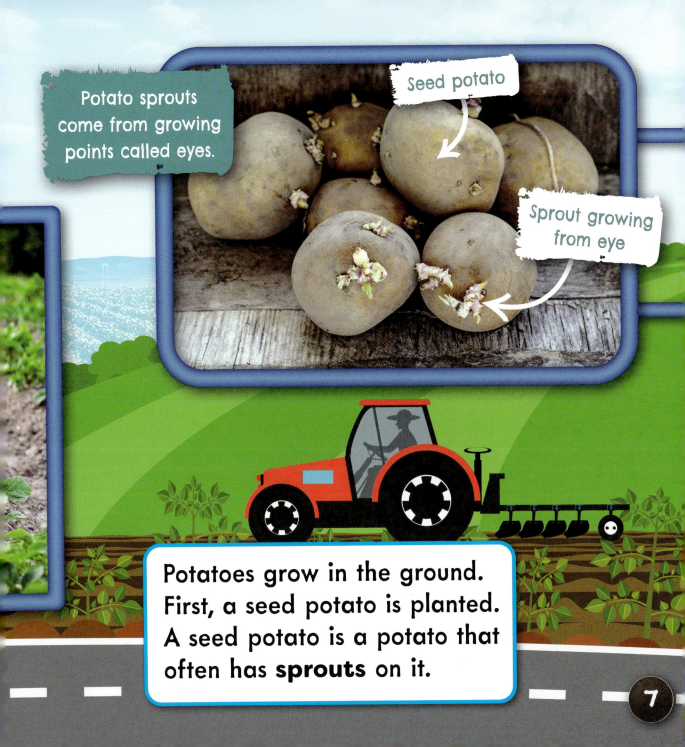

Potato sprouts come from growing points called eyes.

Seed potato

Sprout growing from eye

Potatoes grow in the ground. First, a seed potato is planted. A seed potato is a potato that often has **sprouts** on it.

IN THE FIELD

Before seed potatoes are planted, a farmer must prepare the field. They drive a tractor to make **ridges** in the soil.

Tractor

Ridges

The Potato Patch

When the soil is ready, the seed potatoes are planted. They are placed between the ridges and then covered with soil.

Seed potatoes are usually planted in early spring.

FROM THE ROOTS

Over time, the potato plants grow roots, stems, and leaves.

Leaves

Stem

Roots

The Potato Patch

Root

New potatoes begin to grow from the roots. Potato plants grow flowers, too.

Flowers

Potato

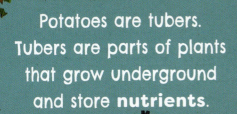

Potatoes are tubers. Tubers are parts of plants that grow underground and store **nutrients**.

READY FOR HARVEST

The potatoes can be **harvested** when their leaves and flowers have died.

The Potato Patch

Each potato plant grows about 10 potatoes.

A tractor drives up and down the field. It digs in the soil and scoops up the potatoes.

PROBLEM POTATOES

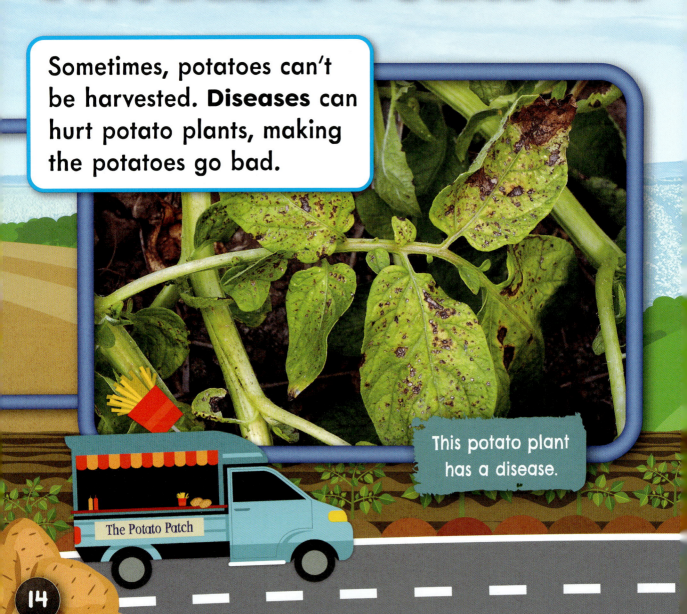

Sometimes, potatoes can't be harvested. **Diseases** can hurt potato plants, making the potatoes go bad.

This potato plant has a disease.

The Potato Patch

TO THE FACTORY

After being harvested, most potatoes are sent to factories to be cleaned.

Some potatoes are not sent to factories. They are sold at farmers markets instead!

The Potato Patch

The potatoes go through a washer that cleans the soil off of them. Then, they are ready to be packaged and sold!

MAKING CHIPS

Some potatoes are made into other foods. A factory that makes potato chips will slice the potatoes very thinly.

The thin slices are **fried** to become crispy potato chips! Then, they are seasoned with salt or other flavors.

A WORLD OF POTATOES

What kinds of potatoes are there, and how are they eaten in different places?

Some potatoes are purple!

Some are long and thin!

Latkes are fried potato pancakes that come from Eastern Europe.

Poutine is a Canadian dish with French fries, gravy, and cheese.

Aloo bonda is a snack in India made from spiced mashed potatoes.

POTATO TIME!

Wow! We've made it back with plenty of potatoes. Now, I can make my yummy food. What would you like to eat?

The Potato Patch

* MENU *

Baked potato with cheese

French fries

Hash browns

Potatoes can be good for us, but fried foods are not. Remember to eat fried foods only as a treat!

23

GLOSSARY

diseases illnesses that cause harm to the health of plants, animals, or people

fried cooked in oil or butter

harvested picked or gathered to be eaten

nutrients things that are needed for plants and animals to be healthy

ridges long, narrow strips of ground where dirt has been pushed up

sprouts plants that have just started to grow

INDEX